Christmas 1969

To Mary Ann,

with Love,

Carol

MORNING
IS
A
LITTLE
CHILD

POEMS BY
JOAN WALSH ANGLUND

HARCOURT, BRACE & WORLD INC., NEW YORK

BY JOAN WALSH ANGLUND

A Friend Is Someone Who Likes You

The Brave Cowboy

Look Out the Window

Love Is a Special Way of Feeling

In a Pumpkin Shell

Cowboy and His Friend

Christmas Is a Time of Giving

Nibble Nibble Mousekin

Spring Is a New Beginning

Cowboy's Secret Life

The Joan Walsh Anglund Sampler

A Pocketful of Proverbs

Childhood Is a Time of Innocence

Un Ami, C'est Quelqu'un Qui T'aime

A Book of Good Tidings

What Color Is Love?

A Year Is Round

A Is for Always

FOR ADULTS

A Cup of Sun

To the Robert F. Kennedy children

KATHLEEN HARTINGTON

JOSEPH PATRICK, II

ROBERT FRANCIS, JR.

DAVID ANTHONY

MARY COURTNEY

MICHAEL LE MOYNE

MARY KERRY

CHRISTOPHER GEORGE

MATTHEW MAXWELL TAYLOR

DOUGLAS HARRIMAN

RORY ELIZABETH KATHERINE

Morning is a little child
      waking from a dream,

Noontime is a yellow cat
      licking yellow cream,

Afternoon's a bumblebee
      on a honey quest,

Evening is a soft gray dove
      winging home to nest.

We built a castle near the rocks,
    we built it out of sand.

Our fortress was an ice-cream box
    with turret, tall and grand.

Our men were twigs, our guns were straws
    from which we'd sipped at lunch.

We had the very best of wars...
    till someone's foot
                    went
                      CRUNCH!

One crocus...

one robin...

one bee...

can
start
a
spring...

you'll
see!

I am walking
just above
the fishes' heads.

Can they see my dark shoe?

Does it make a midnight
in their world?

Are they glad,
in green sunlight,
when I have passed?

I stay within my garden small,
I do not wander past my wall,
but sometimes, when the moon is late,
I wonder what's beyond my gate.

Harbor's hand
    must open wide
to hold so many
        boats inside.

A little train
          rides through the grass
upon a silver rail.
It's just an engine
               and caboose.
The trainman's name
               is
                    "snail."

Hurry, little robin!
          Rain is coming fast.
Leave the tempting cherry bough
          and find your cozy nest.

Shall we have a cup of tea
and a currant bun?

Shall we dance beside the sea
after work is done?

Shall we walk together
    in the twilight gray?

Shall we be the best of friends?
    Shall we start... *today!*

By silver thread
Each moon is led...
A pale, round rainbow thing.

Balloonmen bring us
Each a moon
To carry on a string.

Which is the witch
                that witches?
Which is the ghost
                that stares?
Which is the black cat
                of many lives?
Which is the pumpkin
                that scares?
Where is the goblin
                who gobbles?
Who is behind that mask...?

When it's Halloween and midnight,
perhaps it is best not to ask!

A small speckled visitor
      wearing crimson cape,
brighter than a cherry,
      smaller than a grape.

A polka-dotted someone
      walking on my wall,
a black-hooded lady
      in a scarlet shawl.

A leaf is a letter
      from a tree
that writes, in gold,
      "Remember me!"

Soft bird
    of white
has come
    in night
to hide
    with wings
the gray
    of things.

Bright little winter birds
     coming to feed,
One takes a crumb,
     another a seed.
Each takes a portion,
     according to need.

Good little winter birds,
     teach *us* your creed!

If there were rain or snow outside,
 'twould not be hard to do,

to sit so still, so closed inside,
 as quiet as a shoe,

to sit and bend my head to work,
 to tame my heart and eye,

if it were rainy, or were cold,
 but, oh...a lark flew by!

While I'm in bed,
    the English wake.

While I have lunch,
    their tea they take.

When I say prayers,
    they're sound asleep.

What various clocks
    Our Lord must keep.

What says it's time for March?
Is it the jonquil, bright...
or is it when the first small boy
sends up his paper kite?

Morning glories climb my wall
with small green hands
and never fall.
They sit in bonnets bright and blue
and watch a springtime
make things new.

Though simple is the daisy
and humble is her place,

She smiles at every passerby
and shows a golden face.

A tooth is not supposed to ache,
a tooth is meant to chew,
and so this ache is just mistake...
but, oh...it's hurting too!

I lost myself,
       I can't be found.
I've looked and looked
       around, around.
I've lost myself,
I'm safely hid.
I've lost myself,
       I did, I did.

I have a little germ.
I never meant to get him,
But now he's here
        ...he means to stay!

I guess I'll have to let him.

You cannot hide
        in snow.

No matter where
        you go,

You leave a trail
        behind

That others always
        find.

If I were a robin,
     I'd live here too!

The carpet is washed
     each morning with dew.

The apple trees bend
     in the friendliest way.

If I were a robin,
     I'm sure I would stay!

You are gray velvet,
      you are pink ears,
You are small sounds
      where nothing appears.

You are the nibble
      found in my bread,
You are the scamper
      heard from my bed.

You are the guest
      who's claimed my wee house.
Long tail and whiskers...
      you are
        a
      mouse!

I am a secret
closed up tight.
Knock if you will,
inside is night.

I am a lock
without a key.
I am a puzzle.
No one solves *me!*

"Let me paint your picture,"
Reflection said to Shore.

He caught her likeness in the lake.
It lasted but an hour.

In the summer days
                of sun

Gather seashells
                every one.

In the chilly days
                of fall

Gather apples
              one and all.

In the wintry days
            of snow

Gather snowflakes
            as they blow.

In the daisy days
            of spring

Gather songs
            the robins bring.

The work of water is bubbles!
Day is the job of sun.
Green is the business of gardens,
and the duty of children
           is fun!